Published by Ad Hoc Fiction.
www.AdHocFiction.com

Purchasing Information:
Paperback available from www.AdHocFiction.com
E-book available from all usual outlets.

Printed in the United Kingdom.
First Printing 2020.

ISBN paperback 978-1-912095-14-8
ISBN e-Book 978-1-912095-13-1

Advance Praise

It's astonishing how *The House On the Corner* takes us through eight years of the King family in just forty-five pages. How can a novella in flash have the feel of a saga? Each chapter adds layers to our understanding of the Kings. Woodhouse is skilled at taking her deftly drawn characters and revealing the quiet sadness inside them. There's magic there in what's unspoken. We recognise these people trying to make life work despite the disappointments. This is a tender look at a family; subtle, achy and memorable.

~Sara Crowley, managing editor of *The Forge Magazine*

Deceptive on so many levels, this is a gem of a book. Tiny, it packs a memorable punch as the house of the title oversees a family in ever-deepening crisis. Everyone seeks connection and no one can give it. A subtle, beautifully crafted exploration of misses: missed cues, misunderstandings, missed communication, missed opportunities. A small but powerful litany of the most subtle of destructive behaviours build *The House on the Corner* into a work to care hugely about. Small in stature, big of heart. Not easily forgotten.

~Vanessa Gebbie, author of *The Coward's Tale*

In The House on the Corner, personal tremors large and small unsettle the foundations of a middle-class, nuclear family at the end of the 1980s. Alison Woodhouse has a novelist's gift for capturing in words the currents and eddies of intimate, private thought. Her characters exist in a world of subtle, shadowy shifts – try as they might to understand what's happening around them, they are shaped by forces beyond their comprehension and control. Luckily for the reader, Woodhouse knows exactly what she's doing. She renders her characters' disappointments and joys in paragraph after paragraph of exquisite prose.

~Michael Loveday, author of *Three Men on the Edge*

Alison Woodhouse is a writer who knows her craft. The quiet flashes in *The House on the Corner* are beautifully written stories of missed moments and opportunities not taken. With depth and subtlety, this is a novella-in-flash that warrants repeated readings.

~Diane Simmons, author of *An Inheritance*

The House on the Corner traces the many changes of a London family throughout the mid-eighties and early-nineties. Woodhouse writes with precision and heart, shaking the foundations of a family home while history unfolds outside its door. This is a novella-in-flash that masterfully depicts the intensity of a quiet domestic life.

~Santino Prinzi, author of *This Alone Could Save Us*

THE HOUSE ON THE CORNER

by

Alison Woodhouse

To Claire,
with love,
Alison

For my family, near and far, here and gone, with love.

Contents

All Rivers Must Have a Beginning 1

Wings of Desire. 5

Two Tribes 8

The Next-door Neighbour's Wife 13

On a Dark December Night 17

Song of the Old Mother. 20

A Beautiful Lie 23

Some Other Beginning's End 26

Baking Day 29

Humpty Dumpty 34

Monstrous Green 37

Costing Not Less than Everything 41

In The Uncertain Hour 46

Acknowledgements 49

About the Author 51

All Rivers Must Have a Beginning

The estate agent arrived for the appointment fifteen minutes early. The late Victorian house was on the corner of two roads, one a cul-de-sac and the other a busy artery leading to the heart of the City. She'd visited the house twice before, to draw up the details and take the photographs, and had been impressed by the number of original features: stained glass above the front door, sash windows, intricate cornicing, picture rails and a working fireplace, but there was a patina of neglect overlaying everything like dust. The previous owner had lived there for thirty years, a noteworthy achievement, but the house needed fresh blood. The ancient boiler wouldn't pass health and safety and took up half the bathroom. The windows rattled every time a bus passed by and it would be so much warmer with double-glazing. Without furniture, the rooms should have given an impression of space, but the dark, flocked wallpaper closed them in. She hoped she'd found the right family to bring the house back to life.

She picked up the flyers from the doormat, for pizza delivery and local taxis, and opened a kitchen window to let in fresh air. Maybe she should have brought flowers to brighten the place up? It was February and there was no colour anywhere, just pumice-grey skies and bare trees.

The clients were on time. A young married couple, Helen and Martin King. They'd brought their two children with them, pre-school the estate agent judged, although she wasn't very good at guessing ages. An older boy and a younger girl. The children ran straight upstairs without responding to her greeting, then took it in turns to slide down the worn carpet on their bottoms; up and down they went, up and down, the boy seeming to direct the game without speaking. Their parents let them get on with it.

'It's very old fashioned,' Mrs King said. 'Not quite what I was expecting.' Her husband shrugged. When they'd come to the agency to discuss their requirements, he'd turned up in a smart suit, carrying a briefcase. It was lunchtime and he'd talked fast, listing their requirements, clearly keen to get back to his office. When his wife arrived, flustered and fifteen minutes late, he hardly looked at her. She apologised with a lengthy story about the babysitter and buses, but her husband shook his head and she stopped talking mid-sentence. The estate agent offered her a cup of coffee, but Mrs King said no thank you, she couldn't be away from the children for long.

'It is a bit dark,' the estate agent agreed. 'But that's mostly cosmetic, nothing a bit of decorating won't change. The front of the house is south-facing and very bright, when the sun's out. Would you like to see the bedrooms?'

They followed her. Her boss had told her to watch the body language. Were they relaxed, did they touch each other, hold hands, seem excited? Did they ask questions? Smile? The Kings did none of these things and the estate agent's hopes dipped. Their children had migrated to the bathroom and had climbed into the pink bath. They sat opposite each other, foreheads touching as they whispered. There was a dead spider, legs curled inwards like a clenched fist, which they flicked back and forth and they ignored the adults when they looked in.

'Is there a park nearby?' Mrs King asked.

'Practically on your doorstep,' the estate agent said. 'With a duck pond, garden centre, cafe, swings. It's a lovely spot for families.' She led them to the master bedroom. Mrs King stood in the centre of the empty room and sniffed.

'Has something died?' An unpleasant odour, almost sweet, coated the back of the estate agent's tongue.

'Maybe it's a mouse under the floorboards? You know these old houses.' She wasn't going to tell them this was the room where the previous owner had died. People were funny about things like that.

She was glad to move away from the smell. The two small children had emerged from the bathroom and were waiting in the middle bedroom. The boy shouted for his mother.

'This will be my room,' he said. 'Natty can have the baby room at the back.'

The girl began to complain loudly.

'Don't be silly Joe, it's too big for just you,' his mother said. Now the boy complained too, his voice overriding his sister's. The estate agent saw Mr King look at his watch. She felt a tightening around her temples, an incipient headache. She hoped he could see this house would be a solid investment.

'Shall we look at the kitchen? It might not be to your taste but it's not a difficult job to replace ...'

'You're not kidding,' Mrs King said when they were downstairs again. She had the girl balanced on one hip and the boy held his father's hand. They made a nice tableau, the estate agent thought, framed in the opening that led from the breakfast room to the kitchen. All they needed was a little imagination, a leap of faith and a lot of love.

Wings of Desire

Pink, blue, purple, black.
More black.
Lacy, silky.
Thongs.
Knickers galore.

Helen had never seen such an array of lingerie. She'd discovered them behind the radiator in the guest bedroom when she started to strip the wallpaper, all crusty with dust. She'd put them in a plastic supermarket bag and now Martin was rifling through, a distinct gleam in his eye that she hadn't seen for some time.

'Look at this one,' he held aloft a red satin strip of material. 'Just knickers? No bras? Garters? Stockings?' He moved around the table, his tie loosened, his pupils dilated.

'Didn't the estate agent say an old lady lived here?' Helen said. 'Do you think she had lodgers?'

'Mmmmm,' Martin said.

'What should we do with them? I can hardly take them to the charity shop.'

'I can think of something?' Martin pulled her close. She nearly tripped over a cardboard box. They were supposed to be getting on, sorting out, settling in. There was so much to do to get the house organised. Martin didn't realise how hard it was, the children under her feet all day long. She couldn't get anything done.

'Did you hear that?' she said. Martin dropped his forehead onto her shoulder. There was silence for a heartbeat then the wail of a crying child.

'I'll go,' he said. He kissed her, a butterfly flutter against her lips; leaving only the faintest impression.

Helen had read about relocation anxiety and poor Natalie woke each night with nightmares. She'd started nursery twice a week too. The whole world must seem topsy-turvy. Helen knew how she felt. Joe was stoic, her brave little boy, joining the new primary school, but she mustn't assume he was fine. Boys hid their feelings all the time. She took the bag full of knickers and hid it under the kitchen sink, where neither of the children would find it. She'd put it out with the rubbish in the morning.

By the time Martin came downstairs she'd finished unpacking the crockery. He helped her down from the stool and massaged the back of her neck. She watched their reflections in the kitchen window, ghostly and pale.

'Celebratory nightcap?' Martin asked. He'd given her a bracelet at breakfast, inscribed with her date of birth, July 8th 1955, next to the silver hallmark. Thirty years old. Where was the time going, so quickly?

Two Tribes

Joe said both hamsters belonged to him. Granny had bought them for the children for their birthdays, which were two days apart, but as she'd visited on Joe's birthday, he knew they were really meant for him. He said Natalie could borrow a hamster, but she couldn't choose its name.

He was confident Granny would agree with him. Not cocky, like he heard Mum call him when she was talking to Dad. Natalie had started calling him Cocky Joe. Stupid Natalie. When he pinched her arm she cried just to get attention. Dad said she cried at the drop of a hat. Nat the hat, Dad called her, but Mum always took her side and threatened things like sending him to bed with no tea or making him walk home after football if he couldn't be bothered to say hello when he got in from school. She should stop Natalie being so annoying.

So when she said she'd get rid of both the hamsters if they didn't stop bloody arguing he ignored her.

The hamsters shared a cage in the playroom. Joe and Natalie shared a bedroom. Joe had the top bunk, which was something, but he wanted a room to himself. Mum said they needed to keep a spare bedroom for guests but Granny was the only person who came to stay and that wasn't very often. Now the playroom smelt of the hay at the bottom of the cage, an outdoor smell, not unpleasant, but it made Joe feel itchy and restless.

He'd been home from school for two hours. He'd walked back on his own because Eric and Ben wouldn't let him walk with them. He didn't care. They'd be sorry when he was captain of the football team and didn't pick them. He hopped from one foot to the other, a ball of energy at the base of his spine making his fingers tingle. He poked a paintbrush through the bars of the cage and tickled one of the hamsters. It edged away and crouched at the back of the cage. Natalie had put a thimbleful of hamster food into the cage but already they'd knocked it over, stupid things. Mum had said try apple pips, they'll love them, but either the hamsters weren't hungry or she was wrong.

Natalie was upstairs, having a bath. Joe remembered sharing the water with her, her skin slippery against his, her feet flat against the soles of his, their foreheads touching, playing the staring game, trying not to blink. He nearly always won, even though it made him dizzy. The old bath used to be pink and the carpet used to be soft but now there were cold tiles and Joe didn't let anyone in when he had his bath. He could hear his sister and Mum laughing and splashing.

He wandered into the front room where children weren't supposed to go. It was Dad's room. There was a trolley with dusty glasses and an empty ice bucket. The doors of the corner cupboard above were locked. Joe knew because he'd climbed onto the arm of the sofa once and tried to open it. It was where the bottles were kept.

A large desk stood in the bay window, a leather framed photograph of them all on a beach that Granny must have taken because she always came on holiday with them. Joe couldn't name the place, but he knew it was the last time he'd worn his Liverpool FC cap. He'd discarded it on the sand when he and Nat went rock pooling and then the tide had come in. Dad waded out, even though he didn't have swimming shorts on and Mum said there was no point. Nat held his hand the whole time Dad was in the sea, diving down, coming back up spluttering, shaking his head, unable to locate the cap.

Back in the playroom he studied the hamsters. One had its back turned and its face hidden, the other crouched in a corner. Little black eyes like raisins, a nose that bobbed up and down, white whiskers, tiny paws that looked almost human. The hamster didn't blink. Joe took the paintbrush and poked it again, but it just hunched down even further.

'Have you thought of a name yet?' Joe hadn't heard Mum come in. She crouched down next to him. The hamster cage was on a low table. The two hamsters cuddled together now. They probably didn't like how loud Mum sounded or how close her face was, peering in at them. She put her arm around his shoulders. 'Bad day?' He shrugged her off.

'Eric,' he said.

'And what's Eric's sister going to be called?' she asked. Joe scowled.

'That's not his sister. He doesn't like her. He wants to live by himself.'

'I don't think that's really what Eric wants, do you?' Mum said. The two hamsters were curled so closely together, Joe couldn't see their faces anymore.

Joe woke in the middle of the night. It felt like a giant was shaking their house and he could hear a terrific roaring as the wind hurled itself against the bedroom window.

'Natty,' he leant out of his bunk, hanging his head down. Incredibly, his sister was fast asleep. He climbed down the ladder, crept down the stairs, glad of the light Mum always left on in the hallway.

The hamsters were awake. Eric had an apple pip in his paws and was nibbling fast. The other one was scratching at the base of the cage. Joe sat beside the cage, his back resting against the sofa, and the next thing he knew it was morning and Mum was shaking his shoulder.

Joe stood beside Dad and Natalie on the front doorstep, all of them wearing pyjamas. An enormous branch had broken off the oak tree on The Green opposite and lay half across the road, blocking it. There would be no school, no trains, no buses, no work today. Dad said it was the storm of the century.

'And you slept right through it,' Joe told his sister.

'I didn't. I woke up and I was scared about Lottie, but I knew you'd look after her,' she said.

'Who's Lottie,' Dad asked.

'That's her hamster,' Joe said, wondering how strong you'd have to be to lift up a branch that big and put it back where it belonged.

The Next-door Neighbour's Wife

They'd lived in the house for three years and never had a party. They should have a small get-together and invite the neighbours.

Helen didn't know the names of the family next door. The husband was a doctor, but not at the local practice. There were three teenage children, almost adults. She never heard *them* stamping up and down the stairs or screaming at each other like Joe and Natalie. The next-door neighbour's wife had brought delicious samosas round when they'd first moved in. Martin had answered the door. She wished she'd answered it herself because he'd been quite brusque. People who didn't know him often thought he was rude, which wasn't the case: he didn't like small talk, wasn't very good at it, and after a day at work he sometimes didn't even have the energy to talk to her.

She had baked a Victoria sponge to say thank you but then she'd worried that it wasn't the right thing to do, what if they didn't like sponge cakes or couldn't eat them for religious or cultural reasons. She'd left it in the tin for several days then in a rush of impatience with herself, left the cake on the doorstep with a note.

She shouldn't have put it on a paper plate. If she'd used a real one she'd have had an excuse to knock on the door and get it back. She'd lost an opportunity and it was difficult to create a new one. They were both in their respective houses all day, every day. She could smell frying onions and pungent spices through the thin wall. She could hear the low murmur of the radio. She watched from the bedroom as the next-door neighbour's wife fed her cat or pegged out her washing in their concrete, functional space. She wondered when they'd decided to get rid of the lawn, who had suggested it. She couldn't imagine the conversation at all. There was a large shed, which the doctor used as a workshop. She heard him at the weekend, the whine of a sanding tool. She supposed it was a hobby. She wondered what he made.

Martin didn't have hobbies. She was better able to occupy her free time, so much more of it now that both the children were at school properly. She liked her sewing and had made all the curtains and cushion covers for the house. She thought about making clothes, going to a class, learning to cut her own patterns. Maybe one day, when the children were older and didn't need her but they were still young, only six and ten. If they had a party, she could ask the next-door neighbour's wife to bring a plate of food and they could discuss recipes. Then, when they passed each other coming in or out of their houses, they wouldn't just smile shyly and say hello, they would stop to chat, like friends.

The idea of the party kept her buzzing all day. She made lists of food and drink and thought about how they could clear the furniture from the front room to make space for people to mingle. She spent time standing in the middle of the playroom, wondering if the children still needed a whole room devoted to their toys. They spent most of their time in their bedrooms anyway. When Martin's brother stayed for Christmas and eight of them were squashed around the pine table in the breakfast room, he'd suggested they knock through the two reception rooms, create a big family space, perfect for entertaining. Martin said what would we want that for? His brother said *good old Mart, never changes.*

By the time the children came home from school she was exhausted. The lists, the ideas, the worry. She'd never hosted a party, didn't know where to begin. Surely you had to be friends with your neighbours *before* you invited them? It was presumptuous to assume they'd want to come and if they said no, how mortifying. She began to make the children's tea. She heard quiet activity in the kitchen that mirrored her own, a rattle of saucepans, a cupboard door pushed shut. She put her hand on the beige tiles on the connecting wall, wondered if the wife next-door ever thought about her? But then Joe came in and asked what she was doing and she said *nothing, nothing,* almost shouting.

On a Dark December Night

Martin hooked open the loft hatch and bits of dirt and dead insects rained down. He brushed his hair and face vigorously with his hands, then pulled out the ladder. Downstairs, Helen was playing Monopoly with the children. They'd decorated the Christmas tree, she'd made mince pies. He could have played too, it was a Sunday, but there were jobs to do. She wanted the loft fully boarded so she could store the children's old toys and clothes. Why couldn't they just get rid of them? They weren't having any more, they were both agreed on that. The house was full of stuff, so much stuff, what did they need it all for?

Balanced on the edge of the hatch, he swung his torch around the boxes that were already there. The tape he'd used to seal them had lifted in places. Paraphernalia from a time before they knew each other, items they'd been reluctant to dispose of; as if by abandoning past selves they would be cutting themselves adrift.

He had to feel his way across carefully. At any moment his hand might slip between the joists and punch a hole through the ceiling below. The loft smelt like an aviary. Traffic from the road was muffled. The air was warm, trapped. He reached the first box and eased back the tape. Photo albums, school reports, certificates, letters. In the next box, pictures, medals, shields. He froze when he heard a rustle then a scuttle of tiny claws. He dropped the torch and the light died. Heart hammering, sweat beading his forehead, he felt all around, touching the soft prickle of insulation, roughness of grit and splintering wood. No torch. He shuffled backwards, dragging a box with him. Supporting his weight on his arms he swung his feet over the edge and felt for the ladder. It lurched in its bracket. He began to climb down, taking the weight of the box on his head. He was three steps from the bottom when he felt the ladder lurch a second time, heard a shearing sound of metal snapping. He fell backwards, grappling with the box, landed on his back, his head thumping down on the carpet a second later.

He nursed a brandy in one hand, held an ice pack over the bruise in the other. The children were in bed, Helen reading them a story. They'd been very subdued, abandoned their game and sat quietly one either side of him in the front room. Joe had even said next time he'd go up to the loft and help Daddy. Helen had said absolutely not young man, next time we'll get a builder to do the job. Well that put Martin in his place. Useless at DIY.

The television was on; Wogan had just finished when there was a newsflash. Pan Am Flight 103. Helen had just joined him. She perched on the edge of the sofa, clutched his hand.

'Dear God,' she said, 'Dear God, Martin?' There was a question in her wide, frightened eyes but he couldn't speak; he saw the hole ripped in the side of the aeroplane and heard the noise, the screaming, the air rushing in, sucking out, and he felt as if he was falling, falling, falling.

Song of the Old Mother

Edith was up with the lark, whilst everyone else still slept. The traffic had woken her, it always did when she stayed with Helen, and she couldn't drop off again. She needed her cup of tea and they were out of milk so she let herself out, remembering to take a key, and crossed over the road and the triangle of grass Helen called the Green. Not much of a Green, not like the one in the village with the bandstand and rose garden. She wondered why her feet were so cold: looked down and saw she was still in her slippers. Oh, it was hard, being away from her own home and the children always so noisy, running up and down the stairs, slamming doors, arguing, the boy Joe barging into her bedroom without knocking, the girl Natalie always in tears about something or other. Spoilt, that's what they were. Helen had raised wildlings, which was a surprise because she'd been such a sweet docile little girl herself.

The shopkeeper was surly when Edith didn't have enough money, scornful of the coins in her cumbersome purse with the silver clasp that was harder and harder to open. The price of milk was an outrage. This is London, Helen would say, as if her own mother were a simpleton, a country buffoon. It was sad to think unkind thoughts about your own daughter but Helen was a snob. Ever since she'd married Martin, she'd had airs and graces. What kind of name was Natalie? No one in the family had ever had a foreign name. What was wrong with Jane or Ruth or even Edith?

She wasn't offered a bag for the milk and the slippery carton was awkward to hold with her arthritis but the shopkeeper had already returned to his newspaper and people these days, especially in London, they didn't care, didn't ever think they might wake up one morning with fingers so stiff it was hard to button up your blouse and pain in the evenings that stopped you sleeping. No, so many people these days had no time for a kind word or a helping hand. A young lad bowled into the shop just as she was fumbling for the door, barged straight past, and nearly sent her flying.

He'd left his bike sprawled under the oak tree and Edith almost tripped over it in the half-light. She heard him behind her, footsteps running. His shoulder brushed against hers then he whirled around just in front of her.

'Give us your milk,' he demanded.

She couldn't have heard him right. Her damn hearing going too. But he'd put his hands on his hips and his shoulders back. He was a scrawny thing, skinny, bad skin, a crop of fresh angry spots on his chin and cheeks.

'Give it us,' he said again, urgently, angrily, and made a snatch for it. She struck back, knocking his hand.

'To me,' she said. 'Give it to *me*. Don't they teach you anything in school?'

For a second, he looked impossibly young and as if he might cry. Then he pulled his hood up, hid his face.

'Whatever,' he said, spinning away on his bike, 'fucking old hag.'

Martin was awake when she let herself in, she could hear him in the kitchen, could smell toast. She put the milk on the key table in the hall. Her heart was beating extraordinarily fast. She stepped out of her wet slippers. Her bare feet shrank at the touch of the cold floor. Why couldn't people have carpets these days? Even a rug would be something. Her cheeks were wet, her eyes stung. She climbed the stairs carefully. She didn't want to see Martin or anyone. She didn't think she'd come and stay again.

A Beautiful Lie

'I think the hamster's dead,' Helen told Martin over the phone. She was crouched down beside the cage. The hamster that still lived scuttled to the back of the cage and hunkered down.

'Which one is it?'

'Eric.' Helen wasn't sure. It could be Lottie. Did it matter? There had been two, now there was one, and the children would come back from school and she would have to make them sad, again. This was precisely why she hadn't wanted pets and why her mother should never have brought the wretched animals in as gifts, without asking permission.

'Bloody Mum.' Helen's voice shook. Everyone had been so kind about her, lots of them wanting to speak at the service, but they didn't know what a difficult person she could be.

'She thought she was helping,' Martin said. 'She believed modern children don't confront death and it's better if they grieve less important losses, like Eric, before being faced by the big ones.'

'Well, that didn't work out very well for her, did it?' Helen said. 'Death's everywhere. Think of Christmas, after that plane crash, we couldn't stop Joe watching the news. He was obsessed. Then that awful football match, all those people, crushed? The children know everything, we can't protect them.'

'It's not the same thing,' Martin said. He'd lowered his voice so she knew someone had come into his office. 'If it's on the news, it isn't visceral death. I'm afraid not even your mum was that, they saw a coffin, not a body.' Helen opened the cage door. How visceral did Martin want it to be? Should she leave the poor creature until it started to suppurate? So they could smell death, like that awful stink in the bedroom when they'd first moved in that took months to go, so certainly couldn't have been a mouse under the floorboards, as the estate agent suggested. Martin was still talking. 'I have to go to a meeting. I'll get home as early as I can and see Joe before he goes to bed. I'm sure he'll be okay. He's not a baby anymore and Eric had a good life.'

A good life?

Helen looked at the cage doubtfully. She scooped Eric up. He was already stiff. She found a Tupperware box and put him in it, without the lid, because that seemed a bit too gruesome. She covered him with folded newspaper and held them in place with a rubber band. Luckily the bins were being collected the next day. Then she found the yellow pages and searched for pet shops.

When Joe came in from school he headed straight to the kitchen and the plate of sandwiches his mother always left out. He stuffed one in his mouth and another two in his blazer pocket for later. Then he went through to the playroom to say hello to Eric. Someone had moved the cage onto the floor so he picked it up and put it back onto the table.

'Thanks Mum,' he called out. 'Eric's going bonkers on his new wheel.'

Some Other Beginning's End

Martin couldn't remember the last time he'd been alone in the house overnight. He sat on the hard-backed sofa in the front room, cradling a whisky. Helen and the children were staying at her friend's house for the night, so she could relax, she said, and not worry about driving home. She'd been annoyed he hadn't wanted to join them, but they lived on the other side of London, nowhere near a train or a tube and it would have taken him hours to get there. She hadn't left a note, just a bowl of sausage and tomato pasta in the fridge left over from the previous night's supper. He was glad she hadn't phoned. He didn't want to spoil her evening.

He sipped his whisky, rolled his neck from side to side. He could hear one of the hamsters going round and round in its wheel in the room next door. Round and round. Helen said when those two died she wasn't going to replace them. The children didn't bother about them anymore so what was the point.

He rolled his neck again, drained his glass.

He'd have to tell her they wouldn't be able to extend the mortgage now, so the loft extension was off. His manager said his job was safe, assuming there were no further contractions in the market, but how could you be sure of anything? He wouldn't tell her about that part of the conversation. He'd let her think his promotion was only postponed. He couldn't say they'd appointed a boy only a few years out of Oxford, with an MBA and a smart pinstriped suit. Martin's suits were ten years old and had shiny patches on the elbows and knees. He didn't care, but Helen had mentioned it once or twice, and now he wondered if things like that really did make a difference. And if it did, where did that leave him?

He stood to refill his glass and his elbow caught a photograph on the mantelpiece, knocking it to the floor. His head span when he bent to pick it up. Helen in a frothy dress, him in a hired tuxedo, taken outside the grand old Brixton registry office. Helen's shy smile, her hand tucked inside his elbow. His rather stunned expression, wide-eyed, not smiling. Helen didn't like the photo but said they ought to have an official one framed. He thought she looked nice. They'd married six months after they met. There hadn't seemed any point in waiting. Helen had been engaged before and her fiancé dumped her practically at the altar. Nobody deserved that. Something lurched in him, triggered by the word dumped; he needed to look after her, keep her safe. He'd nearly been engaged himself, had bought the ring and everything. Luckily it was a traditional sapphire and two diamonds — it suited Helen just as much.

The house was very quiet, even the hamster had stopped. He could hear muffled noises from the neighbour's, a television or a radio, and the traffic, a steady stream of cars, but he didn't mind. It was like waves on a pebble beach. Whoosh, whoosh. Helen wanted to double glaze the windows. Something else that would have to wait. Secretly he was relieved. They owed too much already.

His head buzzed, not unpleasantly. He stretched out along the sofa, his almost empty glass resting on his tummy. Helen would say take your shoes off Martin, go and eat your supper. She'd take his glass away, put the bottle back into the cupboard, tell him to go to bed as if he was one of the children.

The hamster started up again, round and round in its wheel. Scrabble and scratch, scrabble and scratch.

Squeak.

Squeak.

Squeak.

Baking Day

The doorbell rang. Helen wished they'd changed it. The chime was embarrassing; the toot toot of a trumpet, and it was set so loud. One of those jobs that had slipped off the list, which had seemed so urgent when they first moved in, like repainting the front door and fitting a bigger letterbox.

It wasn't the postman but a young woman, a lanyard around her neck and a large holdall, which she'd already set down on the doorstep and unzipped. Helen saw a selection of tea towels, chamois leathers, kitchen sponges, scissors, pegs, dental floss, can openers, hot water bottles without covers and boxes of matches. This was the third time in a fortnight. The neighbourhood watch lady had specifically warned residents not to engage with bogus sellers. The charity status hanging around their necks was a scam. There were minibuses waiting at Cockfosters, who brought these people down from Manchester, Liverpool, Leicester, somewhere north, she wasn't exactly sure where, but they were targeting London suburbs because they knew they were a soft touch.

The young woman on the doorstep said hello, her accent Irish. Her front tooth was wonky, her nose was pierced, her hair could do with a wash and a brush, but she had a nice, friendly smile. But before she could speak Helen said, firmly and kindly she hoped,

'Thank you, I don't need anything.'

'You haven't looked,' the young woman's smile slipped. 'I've got ...'

'I know what you've got. I've had two other people like you already. I bought a dustbin and brush from the first one, batteries from the second. So I really have done my bit.' Helen started to close the door but the young woman said,

'Wait, have you got any change? I haven't eaten today.' She was very thin. Helen remembered when she used to be thin, how good it felt to wear tight black jeans and skinny tops. She'd put on at least a stone since Natalie was born and now she was nearer forty than thirty, then she'd be fifty and menopausal and everybody said that made you even fatter. She'd better sort it out now, before it was too late.

'I can do better than money,' she said. 'I've just made cheese scones.' She was so pleased with herself she hurried to the kitchen, forgetting to shut the door and the young woman picked up her holdall and followed her. 'Oh,' Helen said when she realised.

She didn't know what to do, she couldn't order the poor girl out, it would seem so rude and she had just offered her food. 'Why don't you sit down,' she said. 'They're still a bit hot.'

'Can I have a glass of water?' the young woman asked. Helen stopped herself correcting her. This wasn't Natalie thank goodness, not her responsibility, although the girl must still be a teenager. She had a mum somewhere. Did her mum know what she was doing, or where she was? Did she have a home?

'Would you like tea? Or coffee?'

'No thanks, just water. You've got a really nice house.'

'Thank you, we're very happy here,' Helen said and immediately regretted it. It wasn't even true a lot of the time, although it was a nice house. She loved the new kitchen, so modern and sleek but it made her nervous, the young woman eyeing it all up. What if this was what they did, these people, played the victim to scope out a house. Was scope the right word? Martin would think her such a fool, when they were burgled.

'Thanks Miss, that was lovely.'

The young woman was leaving already. Didn't she want to stay, sit in the warm kitchen a little longer, out of the cold? No, she had to get on, she had to try and sell the things in her holdall.

'Will you take some scones?' Helen found a freezer bag in the drawer. She'd made them for a charity fundraiser at school but she'd got plenty of time to make another batch. All day in fact. She counted them out, ten, eleven, twelve, not nearly enough; what else could she give the young woman?

'I do need some more pegs,' she said. 'And a hot water bottle. It gets very chilly sometimes, when it's just me here on my own.'

'Thanks, Miss. Do you want anything for your little girl? I saw the photos in the hall. She looks just like you.'

'Oh she's going to be much prettier,' Helen said. It was true.

'And your boy, is he like his dad?'

'I suppose so,' Helen said, although she thought Joe's character was more like hers. 'Do you have siblings?'

'Uh uh,' the young woman said. 'Just me Mum. She's disabled and can't get to the job centre and the bastards won't give her the dole unless she signs up. It's disgusting.' Helen agreed. She didn't know much about how the system worked. She rooted around in the holdall and ended up buying three more hot water bottles, some hangers, five boxes of matches, three t-towels, two kitchen cloths and a pair of scissors.

'Thanks, you're a brick.' The young woman shouldered her bag.

'Eat the scones while they're warm,' Helen called after her. 'And save some for your Mum.' She wasn't sure the young woman heard, because she closed the door without replying.

Humpty Dumpty

Martin set two deckchairs up at the end of the garden, partly hidden by the buddleia. He nursed his bottle of beer, waiting for Helen to join him.

He was glad to have a few moments. He'd seen Claudia on his way home. Claudia! If he hadn't dropped to his knee and pretended to retie a shoelace, he might have bumped straight into her. She looked exactly the same, power suit, blonde hair in a tight bun, frowning with that funny twist of her lips to the side as she listened to her companion. Unmistakable.

He hadn't seen her since Berlin. He never knew if it was the ring box in his hand luggage or that they'd never travelled together before, but they argued at the airport and didn't speak on the plane and then it was like drowning in quicksand, down and down and down. Of course, there was a final scene when they got home. He couldn't remember what they said, just the unbearable pressure in his chest and head. He remembered the stiletto though. He still had a tiny scar in the middle of his eyebrow, which Helen had noticed the first time they met.

'The kids are waiting for a kiss?' He hadn't heard her coming and spilt beer on his lap. 'Sorry, are you okay?'

'Fine,' he said automatically. 'I'll go up now.'

'They'll be all right for a minute. You don't look fine.' She settled into her deckchair, balancing her glass of wine on the grass by her feet where Martin was sure it would fall over, but it didn't. 'Is it that man at work again? The whippersnapper who took your job?'

'No.'

'What then?'

'There was nearly a fight on the train home. Two young guys having a go at an older man.' He drained half his beer. That wasn't strictly true. There had been some ugly business but it was never going to be a fight and he'd kept his head down, like everyone else in the carriage. Shameful really, when it was so one-sided. He wanted to ask Helen what he should have done, but he knew what she'd say. You did the right thing, don't get involved, it was none of your business. Claudia would have spoken up, he thought, at least young Claudia would, but young Martin would have done exactly the same as he did this evening, and Claudia would have despised him for it.

'What's wrong with people?' Helen said mildly. 'As if there isn't enough trouble in the world.'

They sat in silence for a while. He thought of the Berlin Wall, mostly dismantled now. That wonderful night, three years ago already, when he'd got the kids out of bed, and they all gathered in the front room to watch the news, see the popping of champagne corks, the Trabants hooting, all that hugging and crying, such jubilation. He'd tried to explain something about the history, tried to say he'd been to Berlin, had seen the wall, but Helen said stop lecturing, let them enjoy the moment and she was right.

'Do you want to talk about it?' she asked.

'No, I'm just a bit tired,' he said. She took his hand, held it loosely, stroked his palm with her finger.

'We could have an early night?' she said. She'd become more confident recently, indicating when she wanted sex and how. He was glad, even though he'd been doing it all wrong for years apparently.

Monstrous Green

Natalie dressed carefully in her party clothes, watching her reflection in the long mirror on the inside of the wardrobe door. The girl in the mirror stared back, not blinking. She still had her eyes wide open when Natalie's head popped out of the dress she tugged over her head.

Natalie smoothed the skirt of the dress. It was silky and stuck to her bare legs. Shimmery green, like an iridescent beetle, Mum said. She had done a primary school project on beetles. Most of them only lived for a year and were virtually blind. They used sounds or vibrations to communicate. Mum wasn't interested. They'd found the dress at Granny's house when they went to clear it out, amongst other evening clothes, silky, sparkly. Mum made a funny noise, like a seal barking, pulled it off its hanger and buried her face in it, her shoulders heaving. Back home, she'd told Natalie she would make her the most beautiful dress in the world.

It wasn't beautiful, or maybe it was, but Natalie definitely wasn't. Everyone would laugh at her homemade dress, her snub nose, flat hair, ten-year old ridiculous, ugly self.

The girl in the mirror nodded. *Too right.*

Natalie pulled the dress up over her head, struggling, her arms stuck, sweating.

'Want a hand?' she could hear Mum but not see her.

'You didn't knock!' she tried to shout but her voice was muffled. She felt hands tug on the hem of the dress and the pop of stitches tearing. 'I was trying to take it off,' she said furiously.

'Oh,' Mum said. 'I was going to see if you wanted me to do your hair?'

'Do what with it? It's like straw.'

'That reminds me. It's your turn to clean the hamster cage,' her brother called from his bedroom. 'Eric Three's a bit stinky and Lottie Two won't eat anything.'

'It's my birthday!' Natalie shouted back, outraged. The girl in the mirror glowered. *I hate Joe.* They used to share a room with bunks, his bed above hers. They used to talk when the lights had been turned off. Joe was scared of the dark and always had to be the first one to fall asleep, so he'd make her play twenty questions, who am I? Now he never talked to her, never asked her who she was. She should tell his friends at school what a chicken he was. Then he'd be sorry. The girl in the mirror nodded. *Yeah.*

'What's wrong with the dress, don't you like it?' Mum tugged at one of the sleeves, straightening it. The girl in the mirror caught Natalie's eye. *Go on. Dare you.*

'Is Dad home?' she asked.

'In the garden,' Mum said. 'Setting up the barbeque. Jessie's here, she's helping him.'

Natalie looked out of her window. There was a bald patch on the top of her dad's head that she'd never noticed before. He had changed out of his suit into shorts and his favourite summer shirt, covered in pictures of pineapples. He was blowing the coals, coaxing a flame, holding a bottle of beer. Jessie leant against the fence, drinking from a can of coke, dressed in a halter neck top and a mini skirt. She looked hot. Smoking. Her hair in a high pony-tail, lipstick, eyeliner. Boobs. Something Jessie said made Dad laugh, properly laugh, like she hadn't heard for a long time. Jessie and Dad clinked drinks.

'She looks nice in that dress.'

Natalie spun round, ready to fight, to flounce, to pounce, but her brother was standing in the doorway, talking to Mum, not about Jessie.

'Thanks, Joe,' Mum looked pleased. 'You're turning into quite the little gentleman.' Joe's face flared beetroot and he disappeared. Natalie and the girl in the mirror both laughed. Mum came and stood behind her. She lifted Natalie's hair off her shoulders and twisted it up into a pretend bun. Mum's face was soft and sad and happy at the same time and Natalie felt a queer tightness in her throat, as if she was going to cry, but she didn't know why.

Costing Not Less than Everything

For three whole weeks Martin didn't tell Helen he no longer had a job.

During that time he continued to leave the house at the same time each day, dressed in his suit and tie, carrying his briefcase. He kissed his family, his surly adolescent son, his preoccupied, prepubescent daughter and his distant wife, and walked to the over ground station where, for seven years, he had taken a daily train to his office in the City.

He walked past the station, up the hill, over the footbridge and into the park. He didn't linger, Helen might be meeting friends at the cafe or whatever she did during the weekdays. He didn't have an accurate grasp of her movements, but he knew she spent a large part of the day out of the house. So he walked up the hill, past the woods, crossed over the busy main road, taking no notice of the commuters pouring into the tube station, up another hill, much steeper and by mid morning, because he wasn't a fast walker, had never been a particularly fit or athletic sort of man, he ended up outside Highgate cemetery rather than the Heath, which was where he'd been heading.

He couldn't say what drew him in. At first glance, it was an unprepossessing place. He came at it through a side gate, modestly situated on a dreary urban road, easy to miss. The scale only became apparent once he began to walk up and down the paths, some wide and formal like avenues, others twisty and overgrown. Gothic tombs, many choked by ivy, the stonework crumbling and writing worn to a shadow, an abundance of shrubbery and wildflowers.

There was a smell in the air, damp and feral. He was surrounded by death, decay but something else too: a spirit, an energy, in all the untamed nature flourishing amidst the decaying ruins that belied the gravestones. He was no poet, he didn't read books just reports, statistics, graphs. He couldn't articulate the sensation, but it was as if he was on holiday, absconding, finally free of shackles. It was a conundrum, a mystery and he wanted time to ponder.

In his wanderings, half somnambulant, he came across a particularly large and crumbly sarcophagus, deep along a wooded path. In front, on a plinth, was a full size sculpture of a Labrador lying on its belly and forelegs, chest lifted, head cocked, ears pricked. Someone had tied a red velvet ribbon around the dog's neck. Rufus was chalked onto the stone in neat handwriting. Graffiti or love?

Martin sat next to the dog, his briefcase between his feet. A robin flew down onto the muddy path. He closed his eyes, heard birdsong, a high, pure note and then another, followed by the harsh caw caw of a crow. The wind rustled the treetops. He'd known the recession was coming but he hadn't been quick enough to save his own job. He should have left the bank, got them out of London before house prices started to slip. Risk analysis obviously wasn't the job for him. That made him chuckle, sitting next to a stone dog guarding a stone tomb containing a pile of old bones. Life made him chuckle, when he wasn't at home, in the middle of it. They'd have to sell the house; they couldn't keep up the mortgage payments. He didn't know how to tell Helen. She'd had so many plans. A bigger kitchen, redesign the garden, a loft conversion and he'd always said no, not yet. He stroked the stone dog's smooth head.

'Good boy,' he said.

In the following weeks he came each day and sat by the dog and thought about Helen and what he'd say to her, what she'd say back, what they'd tell the children. It rained and the name Rufus was washed away. No one ever came by. Helen would probably want a divorce. He became sanguine about the outcome whichever way it went, but was still uncomfortable about the process; like seeing a safe harbour surrounded by treacherous waters. He didn't know how to begin but knew he would just have to jump in, strike out.

At the end of the third week, on the Friday, he left in the morning as usual, having kissed his wife and children. He walked to the triangular Green opposite his house and sat on a bench under the horse chestnut. It was late summer and the leaves were turning gold and red and there were conkers on the grass around his feet, some still in their prickly cases, others burst open, gleaming nuts on soft white pillows. He watched his children leave the house, school bags slung over their shoulders, Joe first, so tall and muscular these days, Natalie a few seconds later. She hurried to catch up with her brother but he increased his stride, keeping ahead.

A few minutes later his neighbour, the doctor, emerged. He patted his pockets, tapped his forehead with his fingers and went back inside. When he came out again, his wife was with him. She put her hands on his cheeks and kissed his mouth. Martin, sitting on the bench, felt the warmth of that contact.

His neighbour's wife watched until her husband disappeared around the corner. She looked at Martin and waved. He waved back. They'd never spoken, Martin thought, apart from one time, years ago, when she'd brought some pastries to the house, to welcome them. What a waste.

He stayed a while longer then picked up his briefcase and walked over the green to the house on the corner. He opened the door quietly and paused. It was strange to be home when he should be at work, as if he was trespassing. He put his briefcase down and ran his hand through his hair. He would wait until Helen stopped singing.

In The Uncertain Hour

The estate agent, who'd recently become a partner in the business, arrived at the house on the corner fifteen minutes early.

A junior had taken the photos, drawn up the brochure and conducted the first viewings, but the agent had a particular fondness for this house, her first ever sale. It looked much the same from the outside as it had when she'd first seen it, almost eight years ago. The gate needed painting and so did the front door, but the transformation when she stepped inside was everything she'd hoped for.

There was a large vase of silk white lilies and white roses on the hall table and a bright, fresh, clean smell. She approved of the new kitchen, the open plan living space, the polished wooden floors, the light and airy bathroom. She was pleased for the Kings. The recession was easing at last and the market was picking up. The Prime Minister talked of a new dawn and even if he'd never fill Mrs Thatcher's boots, she had to agree with him. The house had earned the Kings a fair sum, which she guessed they needed now. They were moving near Cambridge. They'd found a cottage with apple trees and a river nearby. It was close to where she'd grown up, Mrs King said when they'd come into the agency to sign the contract, and she wished they'd made the move years ago, whilst her mother was still alive. Mrs King had worn a smart blue skirt and jacket and did all the talking, barely looking at her husband, who sat quietly, one hand resting in the palm of the other.

The doorbell rang, a loud trumpet, toot toot. Though the house was mostly modernised there was so much more a new owner could do with it. A loft extension, landscaped garden, ensuite in the master bedroom.

Mr and Mrs Stearns had brought a small dog with them. The estate agent did not know the breed, she was a cat person, but she said yes of course it could come in though perhaps it should stay in the garden. Mrs Stearns was even larger than the last time she'd seen her, one hand under her belly and the other rubbing the small of her back. The baby must be only a matter of weeks away.

'Oh I love it, just as much as before!' Mrs Stearns said. She kissed her husband and told him to go and measure the bedrooms again, whilst she had a glass of water. He bounded up the stairs two at a time. 'Are the vendors here?' She'd expressed a desire to meet them. People often did, but the estate agent didn't encourage it. She found it strange. A house was not a baton you passed on, but a clean slate, a fresh start.

'I'm afraid not.' The estate agent had gathered from her junior that Mrs King and the children had already moved out and were staying elsewhere and it was Mr King who was dealing with the last bits and pieces. She wondered where he was, whilst being relieved he wasn't around. He'd hardly spoken a word during that last meeting and when she'd shaken his hand to say goodbye, he'd held on a fraction too long.

She wished the best for the Kings, she did for all her clients, but it was her job to find fresh blood, to keep the house alive.

Acknowledgements

Thank you to Jude Higgins for her energy, and encouragement; Ad Hoc Fiction for all the hard work that goes into publication; Michael Loveday, not only for choosing my book, but for his patient, skilful help with editing it afterwards; Jeanette Sheppard for her stunning artwork; Diane Simmons for sensitive critiques and excellent proofreading; Santino Prinzi, Vanessa Gebbie, Diane Simmons, Sara Crowley and Michael Loveday for their generous quotes; the fabulous Flash Community on Twitter and Facebook for their empathy and support; my MA cohort for the feedback and fun; my family for their love and faith in me over many years; and Richard, for everything.

About the Author

Alison Woodhouse lives in the UK. Her flash fiction and short stories have been widely published and anthologised, including *In the Kitchen* (Dahlia Press), *With One Eyes on the Cows* (Bath Flash Fiction), *Leicester Writes 2018 & 2020* (Dahlia Press), *The Real Jazz Baby* (Reflex), *A Girl's Guide go Fishing* (Reflex), *National Flash Fiction Day Anthologies* and *Life on the Margins* (Scottish Arts Trust Story Awards). She has won a number of story competitions including Flash 500, Hastings, HISSAC (flash & short story), NFFD micro, Biffy50, Farnham, Adhoc and Limnisa and been placed in many others. In 2019 she was awarded an MA with Distinction in Creative Writing from Bath Spa University. She helps run Bath Short Story Award, having been a reader for a number of years. When she isn't writing or reading, she loves being with her children, grandchildren, family and friends.